Based on the television series *The Wubbulous World of Dr. Seuss*™.
Produced by The Jim Henson Company, Inc.
Copyright © 1998 The Jim Henson Company, Inc.
THE CAT IN THE HAT, THE GRINCH, and MAX character names and designs
© & TM Dr. Seuss Enterprises, L.P.
THE WUBBULOUS WORLD OF DR. SEUSS is a trademark of Dr. Seuss Enterprises, L.P.,
under exclusive license to The Jim Henson Company, Inc.
All rights reserved under International and Pan-American Copyright Conventions.
Published in the United States by Random House, Inc., New York,
and simultaneously in Canada by Random House of Canada Limited, Toronto.
www.randomhouse.com/seussville/
Library of Congress Cataloging-in-Publication Data
Bryan, Antonia D., 1946–
The Grinch meets his Max / by Antonia D. Bryan.
p. cm. SUMMARY: No matter what the Grinch does,
he can't seem to rid himself of a friendly, playful puppy.
ISBN 0-679-88836-5 (trade). — ISBN 0-679-98836-X (lib. bdg.)
[1. Dogs—Fiction. 2. Behavior—Fiction. 3. Stories in rhyme.]
I. Title. PZ8.3.B8285GR 1998 [E]—dc21 98-7405
Printed in the United States of America 10 9 8 7 6 5 4 3 2 1

GROLIER
BOOK CLUB EDITION

The Wubbulous World of Dr. Seuss™

The GRINCH MEETS HIS MAX

by Antonia D. Bryan

adapted from a script by Will Ryan & Craig Shemin

illustrated by John Lund

Random House/The Jim Henson Company

The Grinch had an itch.
He tried to scratch.
But he could not reach
the itchy patch.

The itch, it tickled.
The itch was ouchy.
It made the Grinch
feel *very* grouchy.

It itched him when he tried to eat.
It itched him when he went to sleep.

It itched him when the snow was snowy.
It itched him when the wind was blowy.

It itched him when the rain was wet.

It itched him when the sun had set.

It made him frown.

It made him roar.

He kicked his foot
right through the door!

The Grinch yelled,

"OUCH!!!"

and grabbed his toes.

Then through the hole...

...there poked a nose!

Into the house
there came a pup.
He gave a yap
and jumped right up.
He cocked his head
and wagged his tail.

The Grinch let out an awful wail!

"Get out, you pup.
Why can't you see?
I'm not your friend.
Your friend's not me!"

"I don't like nice. I don't like funny.
I don't want food. I don't want money.
And if people want to come and chat,
I tell them 'NO!'
And that is *that!*"

The Grinch sat down
to scratch some more.
But once again,
he heard the door.

The pup was jumping
just outside.
His paws were up.
His eyes were wide.
His tail was wagging
quick as quick...
...and in his mouth,
he held a stick.

"Oh, no!" the Grinch yelled.
"Listen, beast,
I do not like you
in the least.
I don't like kids.
I don't like rides.
I don't like cakes
with pink insides.

"When rainbows come,
I shut my eyes.
There's nothing worse
than a surprise.
Parades just make me
run away.
And most of all,
I hate to PLAY!"

He turned around
and slammed the door.
And then sat down
to scratch some more.
And as he scratched,
that Grinch began
to form-u-late...
...an awful plan!
"He wants to fetch?
I'll throw that stick
so far, he won't
get back so quick!"

He tiptoed out
into the yard
and found some ground
that wasn't hard.

And there—
much faster than a mole—
the Grinch began...

...to dig a hole!
He dug that hole
deep as could be.
As deep as sleep,
deep as the sea.

It did not stop.
It just went on
to Hither, Thither,
There, and Yon.
To Upper Milf and Lower Mulf...

...until it came out in the Gulf
of Zitch-a-zulf
(almost as far
as halfway to
the nearest star).

"Hey, pup," he called.
"I'm ready! Come!
I've got a game
that's *really* fun!"

The pup came running
quick as quick.
He brought the Grinch
his favorite stick.

The Grinch said,
"Fetch it! Go! Go! Go!"
He tossed the stick
down low, low, low.

The pup looked down.
He raised one ear...

...then made a jump
and disappeared!

He went so deep
into the dark,
you could not even
hear him bark.

"Yes!" cried the Grinch,
and, without a hitch,
off he went,
to scratch his itch.

He tried to reach it
with a spoon.

He even tried
a fat balloon.

He tried to reach it
with a fan.

He tried to
with a frying pan

He tried to reach it
with a rod
and with a reel
and with a cod.

He tried to reach it
with a boot.

He even tried...

...three kinds of fruit.

He tried to
standing on his head.

He tried to
lying in his bed.

He tried to
on a trampoline.

And with a bright green
Itch Machine.
He tried
and tried
and tried...
...and tried...

...until he just sat down
and cried.

Then all at once,
he heard a sound,

and when he turned
to look around,
the dog was standing at the door,
just as happy as before!

Messy, dirty, tired, and hot,
but back again, no matter what.
Through Mulf and Milf,
through thin and thick,
that dog had come back
with his stick!

"DRAT!" cried the Grinch.
"It just can't be!
That pup still wants
to play with me!

I'll shut my eyes
till I turn green.
He'll see that I am
mad and mean
and bad and nasty
to the core,
and then he'll go
away for sure."

Once more, the Grinch
began to scratch.
(The pup was ready
to play catch.)

The Grinch began
to twist and turn
and wiggle like
a squirmy worm.

The pup looked up
and past the stick,
trotted over
quick as quick.

And then he raised
his two front paws—
and scratched that itch
with nice, sharp claws!

Then all at once
the Grinch felt strange.
Was something new?
Had something changed?

The pup had found
what he could not—
that prickly, tickly,
itchy spot!

And now the Grinch
was not so itchy.
Somehow, he didn't feel so gritchy!
He cried, "Hooray!
The itch is found!
I think you'd better
stick around
until I'm sure
that it is over.

And while you're here,
I'll call you Rover."

The pup looked sad.
He turned away
and wandered off
the other way!
"Wait!" yelled the Grinch.
"Wait, Fido, Spot,
or Bingo, Bongo,
Bozo, Blot!
I'll call you any
name you wish
if you will stay
to scratch my itch."

The pup turned back
and raised his head.
The Grinch could see
a collar (red).

And there he saw
in letters bold
this short word—MAX—
made out of gold.

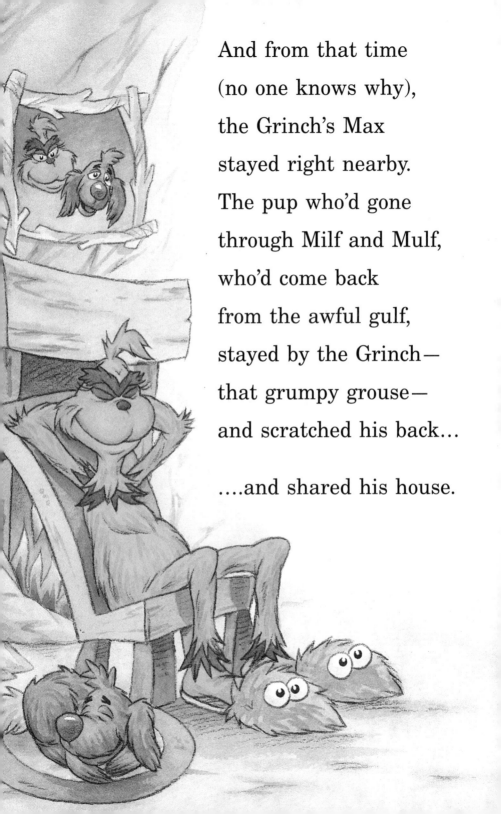

And from that time
(no one knows why),
the Grinch's Max
stayed right nearby.
The pup who'd gone
through Milf and Mulf,
who'd come back
from the awful gulf,
stayed by the Grinch—
that grumpy grouse—
and scratched his back...

....and shared his house.